MISS PRESTON'S PREDICAMENT

A HESITANT MEDIUMS STORY

BELINDA KROLL

Bright
Bird Press

BRIGHT BIRD PRESS

This is a work of historical fantasy, and therefore a work of fiction. The appearance or mention of certain historical figures may be inevitable. Names, characters, organizations, places, events, and incidents are the product of the author's imagination or are used fictitiously. Any resemblance to actual events, locales, or persons, living or dead, is coincidental or historically-inspired. Eerie happenings during Victorian séances are to be expected, do try not to be too alarmed.

MISS PRESTON'S PREDICAMENT
A Hesitant Mediums short story
Copyright 2021 by Binaebi Akah Calkins

ISBN 978-1-7369213-0-2 (pb)
ISBN 978-0-9830786-9-2 (e)
ISBN 978-1-7369213-2-6 (a)

Published by Bright Bird Press at prices that enable the creation of future works. Thank you for respecting the immense energy expended to create the work in your hands.

BELINDA KROLL

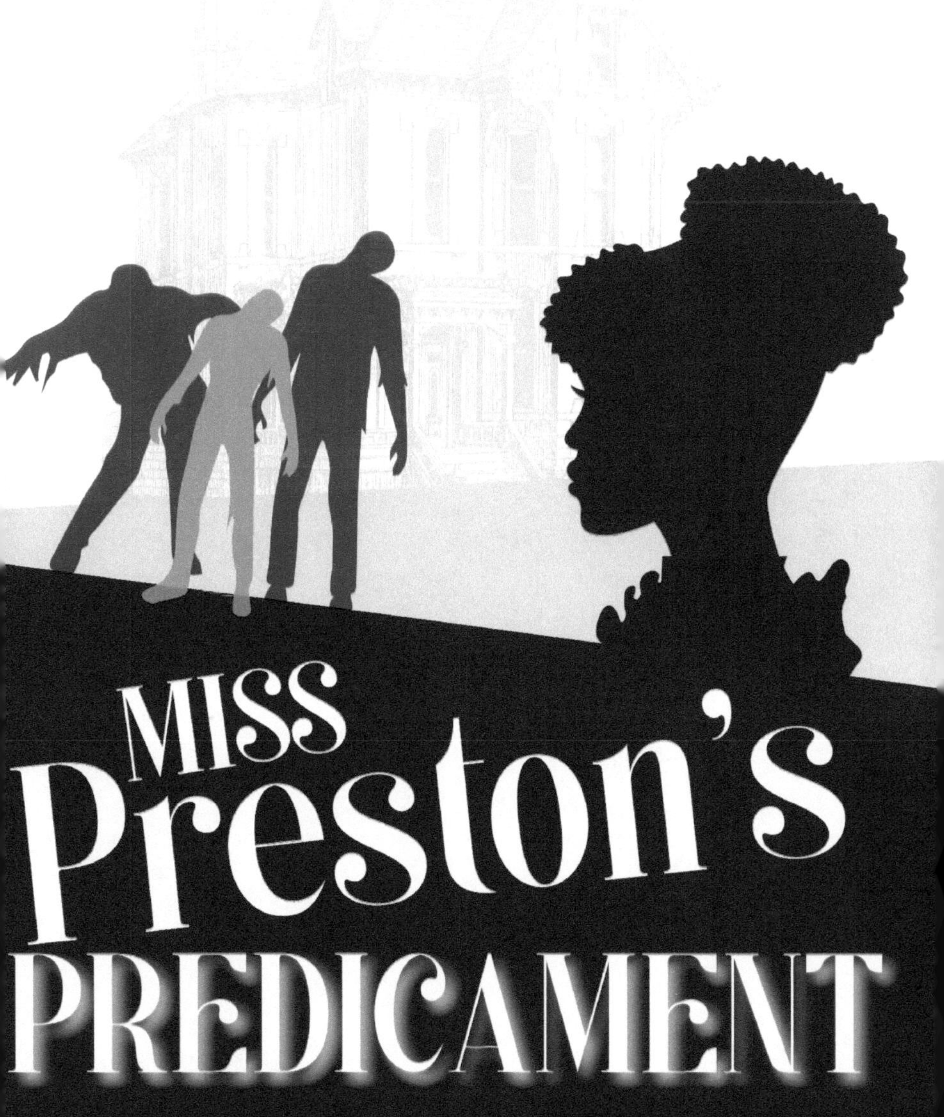

MISS Preston's PREDICAMENT

Author Note
A Hesitant Mediums Story

"Miss Preston's Predicament" is a short story between novels. This story is a standalone referencing characters and events from the historical fantasy romance novel, HAUNTING MISS TRENTWOOD, the first in the Hesitant Mediums series.

ONE

MARYLEBONE, LONDON

JUNE 1887

IT WAS A TRUTH universally ignored, most principally by the dowager Dame Hartwell, that ghosts and gatherings did not mix.

It was one of Dame Hartwell's chief pleasures to host evening spectacles of mediums and spirits. Tonight was sure to be her crowning event, though not for the reasons her attendees might assume. Her steel-blue eyes gleamed with mischief above her ivory cheeks. She signed the last invitation, addressed to a Miss Tessa Preston, and uncle.

It had been a most pleasant surprise last week when Dame Hartwell's informant located her long lost protégé. Five years had passed since Dame Hartwell had laid eyes upon Tessa Preston. She remembered Miss Preston and her uncanny Sense with fondness. At the time, Dame Hartwell had assumed the local Spiritualist Association would welcome them with fanfare.

Unfortunately, Tessa never put stock into the Association, and, in fact, wanted nothing to do with it. Society's wagging tongues delighting over her mixed parentage had been enough to manage: A love match between an Englishman and a Nigerian. It caused Tessa to have a warm terracotta complexion, which always drew eyes her way.

Dame Hartwell never quite knew whether it was the love match or the dissimilar heritages which caused tongues to wag. She was of the mind Tessa should let Society stuff it. Society wouldn't know quality if it hit them in the face, and Tessa was of the finest young ladies. Alas, Miss Preston paid her no mind.

Society had been happy to witness Miss Preston's financial ruin thanks to last-minute modifications to her father's will. Dame Hartwell had searched in vain to help the poor girl. Rather than suffering rumors, Miss Preston ensconced herself in the countryside. She soon left for the Continent with her bachelor uncle, with no assurances of returning.

Dame Hartwell had decided there was nothing to do about it. She focused instead on finding a new medium to sponsor, with very little success. Imagine her delight when her son discovered Mary Trentwood, whose father haunted her! And lo, Mary accepted her son's marriage proposal with a veritable crowd of ghosts hovering about her!

Dame Hartwell's delight was short-lived. Mary refused to perform for séances and continued to pretend she could not Sense the spirits. Disappointment gave way to concern when Dame Hartwell saw the ghosts had ill intent for Mary and her son.

And so it was last week that Mary's butler, Pomeroy, served afternoon tea with his usual aplomb. Pomeroy inclined his balding head toward Dame Hartwell's silver one, winked, and slipped a piece of paper below her teacup. Such familiarity would have caused an uproar in other houses. For Dame Hartwell's piece, Pomeroy's efficiency was a pleasure.

Rumors claimed the Prestons had returned. The slip of paper containing their address was confirmation. Dame Hartwell felt more than a little wicked about inviting Miss Preston to her séance. But needs must, and Dame Hartwell wanted to protect her son and his fiancée from increasingly aggravated spirits. She made sure to include a detail she knew Tessa Preston couldn't resist: the medium conducting the séance was the very same who had swiped her inheritance out from under her.

Dame Hartwell folded the invitation and slipped it into the envelope. She allowed herself a small, delighted giggle.

Two

And so it Begins

Dame Hartwell's parlor

Miss Tessa Preston's concerns were many when she entered the drawing room with her uncle. To receive an invitation for an "evening of quiet observations with the medium, Madam Sylvia" was shocking. To witness guests laughing at their flounces ruffled by impertinent spirits was ghastly.

The cozy room, adorned in velvet and brocades, was set up for an intimate concert. All chairs and settees faced the center of the room. A handsome chaise stood in place of a piano or other such instrument. The garnet-dyed horsehair upholstery gleamed in the candlelight, making Tessa shiver. She was not one to put much weight into portents. Yet, experience taught her that particular shade of red never bade good tidings.

"Uncle Hubert," Tessa said in a dismayed undertone as they found their seats, "tell me I'm imagining."

Hubert Preston, her father's brother, rubbed a tanned hand over the crown of his head, which was also tanned beyond his usual rosy white complexion. He gripped the top of his bone-inlaid cane, remaining silent. He was tall, and though balding, was otherwise at peak health for a man born the year of Queen Victoria's accession. One might have thought his nonchalance all telling. It was the tension in his cane-wielding hand that revealed his thoughts of the situation to Tessa.

Tessa tucked her thin upper lip into her full lower one, musing. She swatted away a naughty ghost pulling a ribbon from her bodice, causing raised eyebrows in her direction. She ignored their looks as she was wont to do. If it wasn't her occasional flailing (an occupational hazard), it was her complexion, a warm brown with olive undertones that tanned golden beneath the Mediterranean sun. She strove to keep her hands in her lap to avoid attracting more interest or suspicion. Tessa wanted above all else to remain nameless until necessary.

Luckily, five years out of Society had taken care of anonymity for her.

Tessa knew she had hardly made waves upon her entry those years ago. Her exit from Society had been nothing more than a couple days' news in the daily rags. Society's short attention span now worked in her favor. They had returned to London with nary a footnote in the paper. In fact, they had been setting up a cozy rental when the invitation landed in her lap. Tessa knew the handwriting immediately. No doubt about it, she had to witness this medium for herself.

Tessa was certain Madam Sylvia lifted monies and jewels rather than spirits. She doubted Madam Sylvia had any inkling of the Sense. It would take all her patience to assess the woman's awareness of the Sense before revealing her as a fraud.

Tessa did her best to ignore the ghost who picked at the posies tucked in the intricately arranged braids that structured her black, tight, corkscrew curls into the fashion of the day. Her mouth couldn't help but make a moue of annoyance. The ghost flicked her pearl earrings and whispered inappropriate suggestions—of which he could do nothing about—into her ear.

Uncle Hubert, seeing Tessa's increasing distress, stomped the foot of his bone-inlaid cane against the tiled floor thrice. He muttered the words Tessa had instructed him to for moments like these.

The ghost hovering over Tessa shuddered, hearing reverberations no human ear could discern. He lurched in the direction of another young lady who unfortunately lacked the Sense. She was ever so embarrassed when the ghost upended her reticule to the floor. Two gentlemen seeking her favor rushed to her aide. Their enthusiasm waned upon discovering her dance card was pre-filled with their names. The notes beside their names were hardly flattering.

The ghost, pleased with his antics, joined two spirits lurking in the far corner of the drawing room.

Tessa's dark eyes danced as nodded her thanks to her uncle. Uncle Hubert winked and resumed his feigned nonchalance. No longer distracted, they scanned the room. It seemed they would not get a glimpse of the medium before the evening began.

"Do you think it's the same woman?" Tessa murmured to Uncle Hubert.

Uncle Hubert harrumphed, unwilling to speculate with Dame Hartwell sweeping into the room.

THREE

PREPARATIONS AFOOT

DAME HARTWELL KNEW AS soon as she stepped into the room that Tessa had fallen for the bait. The looks thrown from her regular séance attendees gave her a point in the room upon which to focus. Tessa and her uncle sat in the second row of seats. They did not make small talk, keeping very much to themselves. Such a shame, because despite her pragmatic nature, Tessa was good at social niceties. Dame Hartwell remembered remarking upon Tessa's impeccable manners once.

Only later did it occur to her that they were necessary to combat the prejudices against Tessa.

Tessa was, of course, as beautiful as ever. Her wide, dark eyes glowed in anticipating of the evening's events. The pale-yellow gown she wore was a handsome complement to her mahogany complexion. She wore her black curls twisted and braided into an intricate pile atop her head. Posies accentuated the impressive coiffure. Dame Hartwell could tell with her own meager Sense skills that Tessa shimmered. She knew Tessa had heard many a life story over the years, from persons drawn to her despite their prejudices.

Having a heart open to ease pain made Tessa the ideal medium, both for the living and the departed. It was an innate skill, and one Dame Hartwell hoped she could align with her own needs.

Not wanting to seem as though she stared at the Prestons, Dame Hartwell continued her sweep of the room. She was able to Sense three ghosts in the corner, fewer than usual.

A quick glance at the evening's attendees explained why. Dame Hartwell's son, Alex, had taken his fiancée Mary out to the theater to avoid the séance. It also meant the usual crowd of spirits had followed them instead of hanging about the house.

Dame Hartwell touched the lace cap perched atop her silver hair, ready to start the evening. She needed to know for certain that Tessa maintained her Sense if she wanted to hire her as a guard for Alex and Mary. She noted the color of Tessa's dress and whispered it to Madam Sylvia, hiding out of view.

Oh, how she hoped this would all work out as planned.

Four

Madam Sylvia

Tessa couldn't believe how well Dame Hartwell seemed since she last saw her five years ago.

Dame Hartwell was a small woman with delicate features. Following the queen's example, she wore a gray dress out of perpetual mourning for her husband. The color complemented her soft tones: her blue eyes snapped; her silver hair gleamed. Her petite stature and pleasant behavior were a façade to her formidable will. Tessa choked on the memories washing over her.

A stately butler walked around the room, dimming the gas lights. Dame Hartwell herself lit five candles on tall staffs arranged in a circle around the chaise. It was all nonsense, and the ghosts knew it, tittering amongst themselves in the corner.

Dame Hartwell commanded attention with a solemn thwack against a metal gong.

Tessa pressed her lips together against a chuckle. She didn't dare look at Uncle Hubert, who would encourage impolite behavior for his own entertainment.

"Ladies and gentlemen," Dame Hartwell said. "I am beyond pleased to share with you the exquisite talents of my guest of honor, the medium, Madam Sylvia."

Tessa allowed herself a congratulatory smile. Finally, after all these years.

The cliché "Madam Sylvia" swept down the center aisle, parting the rows of audience chairs. Tessa leaned forward in her seat, studying the woman as she walked past. Bile rose in Tessa's throat as she realized this had to be the woman who came to her home five years ago. Madam Sylvia had auburn hair, green eyes, and smooth skin that romantic authors would describe as alabaster.

Madam Sylvia wore all black but for the gossamer robe she draped atop her bustled and flounced gown, which was an unlikely shade of red. Madam Sylvia arrived at the chaise in the center of the room and laid herself in a seductive lounging position.

Tessa wondered how much of her inheritance went toward buying such garish clothing. She did her best not to grind her teeth.

Madam Sylvia leaned back into the chaise. Most mediums were models of prim femininity. A commonplace medium used her advantage to demand votes for women and similar social justices. In contrast, Madam Sylvia delighted in titillating her audience. She wore her bodice cut low. With her artful positioning, it was as though she might fall out of it.

The responsive murmuring made Tessa glance around the room. It seemed she, and Uncle Hubert, of course, were the only ones keeping their wits. Tessa's lip curled. Why had Dame Hartwell thought to invite her to this spectacle? And why had she decided to come?

"I sense a spirit," Madam Sylvia moaned. She lolled her head from side to side and up and down. "Spirit, tell me, is there someone in the room with whom you wish to speak?"

It was clear Madam Sylvia meant to give everyone a show. The audience, as one, leaned forward, eager to contribute.

Tessa, bored and unaware of Dame Hartwell's watchful eye, began counting the ghosts in the corner. There were three gentlemen of varying ages and formal dress.

The youngest was around Tessa's age, not yet thirty. He wore tight calfskin breeches and a floral waistcoat. He styled his hair tousled in the style of the Regency. He was the flirt who had caused all the ruckus upon their arrival. Though annoying, Tessa found herself pitying him. He must have died having too much fun. He was now doomed to observe others until he found someone who could help him on his path Beyond.

The other two ghosts faded in and out of sight, even for someone with an attuned Sense like Tessa. It was likely they had been ghosts for so long that they had forgotten what it was to be alive. Thus, they felt no compulsion to maintain their shape for more than a few minutes at a time.

Tessa blinked three times and shook her head to pull out of Sensing their presence. She glanced about the room, wondering if anyone happened to see what she did. She knew there was very little chance that Madam Sylvia had any idea about the ghosts in the corner.

Madam Sylvia wailed, making Tessa jump.

Uncle Hubert chuckled. "You're missing quite the show," he whispered.

Tessa was mid-eye roll when she realized everyone stared at her.

"The spirits wish to commune with the soul in yellow," Madam Sylvia said, louder and more pointed this time. "A young soul, bright and golden, adorned in yellow, cries the spirit!"

With growing horror, Tessa realized she was the only woman in the room wearing any shade of yellow. She swallowed her annoyance at Madam Sylvia calling her "young." She was past her season for years. What did Madam Sylvia mean by teasing her so?

Dame Hartwell looked about the room, her steel blue eyes landing on Tessa with glee. "Why, it's Miss Preston."

Tessa kept her smile polite and tight as her father had always instructed her. How ridiculous. What game was Dame Hartwell playing by acting surprised to see her? They had received her personal plea to attend.

The room filled with murmurs. Hadn't there been a Miss Preston years ago? An heiress to a wealthy merchant who bought his daughter's entry to Society? Hadn't she lost the estate to a medium? Hadn't there been some scandal surrounding her parents' deaths?

Tessa's lips thinned. Uncle Hubert pulled her hand through to rest inside his elbow, patting it in place. Once again, Tessa wished the incantation embedded in his cane worked on the dead *and* the living.

"Come forward, Miss Preston," Madam Sylvia said. She dropped her voice back into a dulcet huskiness as she waved her hand in a languid manner.

It took every ounce of self-control to not exchange an incredulous look with her uncle. Tessa smoothed her skirts, stood, and patted her uncle on the shoulder. It was her unspoken promise to not cause too much trouble if her annoyance got the best of her.

Madam Sylvia held out her hand for Tessa's during her approach. Dame Hartwell, in the meantime, had reclaimed her seat nearest to Madam Sylvia.

Tessa had the uncanny feeling of experiencing this before. She locked eyes with Dame Hartwell, wondering again why the invitation. Dame Hartwell's expression betrayed nothing beyond excited anticipation. It filled Tessa with dread.

Tessa made a point of sitting on the end of the chaise, down by Madam Sylvia's feet. She watched Madam Sylvia, hoping she seemed unimpressed. The audience's gaze upon the both of them was neither amused nor entertained. Tessa was certain the attendees were jealous. If she were feeling uncharitable, she might have even said the room had turned feral.

Madam Sylvia smirked, knowing that angled as she was on the chaise, the attendees could not see. All they saw was a rigid posture, lolling head, and her husky voice. "The spirits call to you, Miss Preston!"

Tessa imagined all the ways in which she could reveal Madam Sylvia's ineptitude. She let her gaze sweep over the room, playing along for now. "What do the spirits want of me?"

When Madam Sylvia did not respond, Tessa turned to her, ready to witness more inane dramatics. What she saw instead gave her a start.

Madam Sylvia bolted upright, her spine rod straight. She threw her head back so that her careful auburn coiffure fell to her shoulders. Her hands clawed at her neck in a gentle, hypnotic manner.

The audience held their breath after a collective, horrified gasp.

Tessa leaned toward Madam Sylvia, careful not to touch her. She allowed her Sense to open, incredulous though she might be. She needed to know whether Madam Sylvia was a medium or an excellent actress.

It took a moment to see beyond the point of seeing. Tessa sensed translucent ribbons tightening around Madam Sylvia's neck. The ends of the ribbons trailed out into the ether. It was impossible to tell who hijacked Madam Sylvia's ability to speak.

An actual spirit had caught Madam Sylvia unawares. A powerful one not located in the room, from what Tessa could discern. She would have laughed if the situation hadn't turned so dangerous.

"Sylvia?" Tessa said.

Madam Sylvia did not respond at first. Her head fell forward, and unseeing eyes stared back at Tessa. A voice erupted so unlike her own that it must belong to someone else. "Tessa. Tessa, baby."

Tessa stood, dropping her purse to the floor as she backed away. "That's not funny." Only her mother had ever spoken to her in such a manner, and she had been dead these five years.

"Tessa. Baby," Madam Sylvia repeated. She no longer sounded sultry. Her voice deepened. Certain syllables received a slight emphasis, making her sound musical, and quite foreign. She held out a hand for Tessa. This time it was a gesture of welcome and tenderness instead of arrogance and bravado.

From the corner of her eye, Tessa saw her uncle stand, holding his cane at the ready.

"Tessa, baby," Madam Sylvia repeated. "Tessa, baby, they know about you."

Others in the room began to shift in their seats, unsure what their part would be in this scene. Tessa noted the behavior of the crowd as confirmation they had never attended a proper séance. While unnerving and upsetting, this was actually rather routine.

"Tessa, baby." Madam Sylvia leveled her unseeing gaze at Tessa. "They know about you, and they're coming."

Tessa knew she ought to take Madam Sylvia's possessed words for the ominous warning they were intended to be. Tessa instead fixated on the fact that Madam Sylvia was a real medium.

What a bother.

FIVE

BACK TO BUSINESS

DAME HARTWELL, HAVING SAT back long enough, stood with an inscrutable expression. She had intended for Madam Sylvia to ask a couple questions of Tessa. She had wanted Tessa to reveal her talents with the Sense, maybe even entice one of the spirits to force Tessa's hand.

Instead, Madam Sylvia proved a theory Dame Hartwell had always harbored about Tessa. Elated by the development, Dame Hartwell knew she needed to control the situation. Out of all the séances she had hosted, she was certain this was the first time a real spirit had spoken through her medium. It was rather more dramatic than the usual palm reading and horoscopes.

Dame Hartwell held up her hands to placate the annoyed audience.

"My dears," she said, her smile both electrifying and arresting. "I fear we must adjourn for the evening."

At first, the audience stared at Dame Hartwell, disbelieving. Then, as of one mind, everyone but her uncle glared at Tessa. They began voicing their displeasure that some nameless, foreign-looking woman received Madam Sylvia's attention.

"Come, come, if you would remove the… negative influence… we can continue with our program," called a voice from the crowd.

"I do hope this was not all a ruse, my lady," came another voice. "I contributed handsomely to you, to further the advancement of Spiritualism. I intend to see the fruits of my donation!"

Tessa bit the inside of her cheek, focusing on the ribbons wafting behind Madam Sylvia's throat. It was mortifying that the crowd was far more upset by her presence than the possession. It seemed possessive spirits were not nearly as disruptive as she.

Dame Hartwell was firm. "No, my dears, we cannot. The spirits are unhappy. I doubt they shall entertain our questions this evening any further. Do wait for an invitation for another soiree. Indeed, depend upon it. We shall see one another soon."

The manservant who had dimmed the gas lights not an hour ago began guiding everyone out.

Dame Hartwell clapped her hands when only Uncle Hubert, Tessa, and an unresponsive Madam Sylvia remained.

Her clear delight was off-putting, and Tessa's earlier fury melted into a wary sort of concern. It had been five years, after all. Perhaps the lady's mind wasn't what it once had been.

"Well, isn't this just!" Dame Hartwell said, gesturing at Madam Sylvia. She rounded on Tessa, who had been inching to the door with her uncle in tow. "And look at you!"

Tessa froze as Dame Hartwell, in her demonstrative and irregular manner, embraced her. "My lady."

"I had so hoped you would be unable to resist my invitation," Dame Hartwell said. "You know, I hosted Madam Sylvia to pull you out of the woodwork."

Tessa and Uncle Hubert exchanged uneasy glances. "Whatever for, my lady?" Uncle Hubert said.

"To test my theory!"

"Theory?" Uncle Hubert said.

"Why, that Miss Preston is an excellent amplifier, of sorts."

Tessa frowned. "Amplifier?"

"Look at poor Madam Sylvia," Dame Hartwell said. "She has no idea how to escape her trance, as she's never fallen into one on her own." The cackle that emitted from Dame Hartwell caused them to step back out of dismay.

Tessa clicked the clasp of her purse open and shut to avoid wringing her hands. "Nonsense," she said. "I've encountered Madam Sylvia before. She cheated me out of my inheritance through tricks, not the Sense. I would have known."

Uncle Hubert rubbed his chin. "You know, my dear, Dame Hartwell has a point. Your father came under her influence once you entered the room to proclaim her a fake. He had been quite refusing to sign anything up until that point."

Tessa shook her head. "But then that would mean I cheated myself! That I *gave* Madam Sylvia the power to hypnotize my father? Impossible."

"Improbable," Uncle Hubert corrected, "but not impossible. What have we been doing these recent years but testing your skills? How odd has it been, that we only ever find those attuned, or lacking any Sense at all?"

Odd indeed, and something Tessa had wondered about herself. She had dismissed the coincidence as some odd quirk of being on the European continent. Their travels had taught them much about how to control Tessa's Sense. They learned very little about the origination of the peculiarity. They had no idea whether other mediums had the same sort of constraints as she experienced.

Tessa rubbed her forehead. "And now that you've confirmed your theory, what is it that you want, my lady?"

Uncle Hubert inhaled, not accustomed to Tessa speaking so to the aristocracy. True, Dame Hartwell was the lower aristocracy, being the widow of a knight. Yet, she was aristocracy, and could be their ticket into the Spiritualist Association. He narrowed his eyes at Tessa, warning that she minded her manners.

"Why, nothing of great import," Dame Hartwell said. "I mean to hire you on retainer. You shall ensure my evenings are a success!"

Tessa's jaw went slack. Her uncle was unable to choke back his exclamation of surprise.

"You must know I've been attempting to entice you for years. Almost as soon as you lost your inheritance and left our circle," Dame Hartwell said. "Oh, dear Florence shall be quite excited to have you about again. She always did enjoy the adventures you inspired."

Tessa remembered Florence, Dame Hartwell's daughter and her peer during her Season. A blonde, nervous girl who accepted the first man who proposed to avoid the anxiety of waiting the entire Season, Florence was hardly what Tessa would have called "adventurous."

"Tessa has yet to accept, my lady," Uncle Hubert said.

Dame Hartwell waved her hand. "She will. She is. She's too sensible a girl to refuse such an opportunity."

Tessa glared, unable to say anything to the contrary for Dame Hartwell spoke the truth. They needed the money. And this had the added benefit of legitimizing her with the other lower aristocracy. She wouldn't feel the need to hide her Sense. With Dame Hartwell's patronage, no one would dare label her a foreign witch-woman.

Tessa shook her head, knowing Dame Hartwell had to be enjoying this. She knew Tessa had come here to confront Madam Sylvia. She had even hoped to reclaim the remainder of her fortune, however modest it might have been. Yet now it seemed Dame Hartwell was offering her a new fortune. A new future.

Unable to concentrate with Madam Sylvia staring at her with those blank eyes, Tessa knelt. She frowned as she realized Madam Sylvia's mouth moved. She leaned closer, hearing her name repeated over and over again.

They had seen much on the continent, Tessa and Uncle Hubert. Their lives had been at risk more than once. Yet none of their adventures had prepared Tessa for hearing her name on repeat from Beyond. Chills ran down her spine. She studied the translucent ribbons whose ends disappeared into nothing. She reached out to touch one.

The three ghosts in the corner, silent up to this moment, began screeching. They lurched forward, causing Uncle Hubert's coattails to fly and Dame Hartwell's skirts to reveal her ankles. They threw Tessa. She landed on her back, crushing her bustle, knocked breathless.

It took a moment for Uncle Hubert and Dame Hartwell to regain their wits. Tessa blinked at the intricate molding on the cream ceiling. Cupids.

How banal.

Tessa pushed up onto her elbows. "Well, that was rude." She accepted Uncle Hubert's hand and wiped her backside upon standing again. "I can't say I've ever had that happen before."

Dame Hartwell's excitement faded now that her ghosts weren't in a flirting mood. "Do ghosts often behave like this around you?"

"We do have an unfortunate impact on their gentility," Uncle Hubert said.

"Yet, we've never had a welcome quite like *that* before," Tessa mused. She studied the ghosts prowling over the swaying Madam Sylvia before eyeing Uncle Hubert's cane. It had been a gift from a group of Roma that they had helped over a year ago. Their seer, newly deceased, had taught her the protective words to use. With those words came the warning to return home, for there were spirits gathering in England with ill intent. Surely these three ghosts were but a taste of what was happening across the country.

Tessa bit the inside of her cheek, decision made. While the cane held a quiet power unto itself, when she held it…

"My lady," Tessa said, "you'll have to excuse my impertinence."

Before Dame Hartwell could ask what she meant, Tessa grabbed her by the elbow and shoved her across the room. With a deft spin, Tessa caught the cane Uncle Hubert threw at her. She pointed it at the three ghosts.

The two ghosts who had not bothered keeping their shape for more than minutes now eyed her. Their forms grew large and menacing. The ghost of the Regency dandy hung back, compelled to protect Madam Sylvia. He did not seem to understand why and was not altogether enjoying the experience. Tessa could relate.

"You cannot harm us," rumbled a low voice from the leftmost spirit.

Tessa quirked an eyebrow. "Spoken like a brute. What makes you think my first inclination is to harm you?" She whispered the start of a phrase that would release their spirits to their awaiting judgment.

The two larger forms lurched at Tessa, this time making contact. One gave up all pretense at human form, snaking around her neck and squeezing. The other tried yanking the cane from her. Tessa fought them, snarling. The snarls quite shocked Dame Hartwell, who fell back with a hand upon her bodice as her mouth hung ajar.

Uncle Hubert came beside Tessa, his hands around hers to steady the cane. "What can I do, m'dear?"

Tessa wheezed. The spirit took advantage and wrapped tighter around her throat. She, with Uncle Hubert's help, pulled at the cane, fighting with the second spirit to point it at herself.

"Is this wise?" Uncle Hubert asked. They had never tried the cane on themselves.

Eyes bulging, Tessa didn't care. She rasped the last word from the phrase. She felt more than heard the spirit around her neck shriek. The dispersal spell yanked the spirit down between the floor tiles. Tessa stumbled, gulping air. The second spirit released the cane and disappeared through the ceiling.

The dandy spirit stared beside Dame Hartwell, who sported a similar expression. "Right," he said, and walked out of the room with all the grace and pride one can manage when scared witless.

SIX

A NEGOTIATION

"…INCREDIBLE," WAS ALL DAME Hartwell could think to say.

Dame Hartwell was all agog as Tessa fought the spirits she had suspected were haunting her house. She had known, of course, that they were not pleasant spirits. She had never imagined they would attack anyone!

Well, that wasn't entirely true. Dame Hartwell had *hoped* they wouldn't attack anyone. Yet her recent nightmares had prophesied something similar happening. How chilling.

Dame Hartwell rubbed her fingertips against her temples, warding off a headache. "What do you suggest we do with Madam Sylvia?"

Tessa tugged at the hem of her bodice. "This is the easy part."

Dame Hartwell stood aside, gesturing for Tessa to continue. Tessa's confidence was astounding. This was no longer the reticent young woman she had once watched over. Tessa's time on the continent must have included a fair amount of spiritual encounters. The experience gave her the same forbearance of a duchess.

Tessa knelt in front of Madam Sylvia again, placing her hands on either side of Madam Sylvia's face. She still murmured Tessa's name, but now tears streamed down her face.

"Your parents are proud of you," Madam Sylvia whispered in her own voice before continuing to murmur Tessa's name.

Tessa stiffened. "You are never to speak of my parents again." To the gray ribbons wrapped around Madam Sylvia's throat, she said, "Your warning arrived, thank you. Release this woman, if you please."

Madam Sylvia slumped forward into Tessa's arms. With an unladylike grunt, Tessa arranged Madam Sylvia on the chaise with not too gentle a touch. She stood, smoothing her skirts.

"Well," Dame Hartwell said. "I don't suppose you've considered my offer? You'll not find a house more worthy of your... attention."

Tessa returned the expectant expression of her uncle with one of her own. If someone or something was coming for her, she would do better to face it with resources.

"I would never want to contradict you, my lady. Of course, I accept." Tessa smiled, hoping she wouldn't one day regret it.

Dame Hartwell clapped her hands. "Quite the thing. You must stay for refreshment, I insist. Do not think of the late hour, you broke up my party early enough. Pomeroy will tend to your things."

"Our things?" Tessa said.

"I can hardly keep you on retainer if you aren't living here. There is an odd collection of ghosts here, my dear, and you are the person to handle them."

Tessa exchanged a glance with Uncle Hubert.

Dame Hartwell, noting the creeping distrust, was quick to say, "I will double your pay if you live here. And I will sponsor your entry to the Spiritualist Association."

Uncle Hubert spun his cane. "You've done your research. I'm certain when you last spoke with Tessa, she had no interest in the association. What makes you think she changed her mind?"

"One doesn't gallivant across Europe to return to London for a quiet life," Dame Hartwell retorted. She took Tessa's hand. "I insist, you must remain under this roof for my purposes."

"That's exactly my concern, my lady." Tessa kept her voice soft, though there was no mistaking the hardness in her eyes. "I never know your purposes until it's too late."

Dame Hartwell waved her hand. "Pish posh, do not drag our history into this. I need your answer now."

Tessa sighed. "Of course, my lady. I'm sure you already know where we are staying, since you sent the invitation. If you wouldn't mind paying the rest of the week's rent, we'd be much obliged."

Uncle Hubert coughed, his face turning red. He never did like to discuss such vulgar things as payment, and gladly left it up to Tessa.

Dame Hartwell smiled. Crowning achievement, indeed. She was sure to sleep well tonight, no matter how many of those nasty ghosts decided to swirl around her family. With Tessa's unique Sense abilities, what could befall Alex and Mary?

Message from the Author

I hope you had as much fun reading this as I had writing it. If you liked this book, please consider writing a review at one of the locations below. As an independent author, your reviews and word-of-mouth are key to the success of this book and my writing career.

Website https://worderella.com
BookBub https://worderella.com/bookbub
Goodreads https://worderella.com/goodreads

Become a VIP

If you would like to be contacted when I release a new work, subscribe to my newsletter or become a patron of my community, the Cozy Coterie. Cozy Coterie patrons receive discounts from my store, including exclusive editions.

Newsletter https://worderella.com/vip
Cozy Coterie https://worderella.com/cozycoterie

WANT MORE?

28

Read more about Tessa, Uncle Hubert, and Dame Hartwell in A SPIRITED ENGAGEMENT, the second book in the Hesitant Mediums series.

TITLES BY BELINDA KROLL

HESITANT MEDIUMS

Haunting Miss Trentwood
Miss Preston's Predicament (story)
An Inconvenient Séance (story)
A Spirited Engagement

OTHER TITLES

The Last April
Catching the Rose

Beatrice Learns to Dance
as Binaebi Akah

HAUNTING MISS TRENTWOOD
BOOK 1 OF THE HESITANT MEDIUMS

It was a truth universally acknowledged that one's suitors and ghosts ought never mix, especially when the ghost was one's father.

Resigned to spinsterhood in her English manor house, Mary Trentwood is horrified when her father's ghost crawls from his grave, and struggles as he spouts opinion after opinion about the *most mundane* things.

Mistaking the newly-arrived and quietly handsome Alexander Hartwell as her father's solicitor—for who else would interrupt her mourning?—Mary soon realizes her father is adding matchmaking to his repertoire. Neither Mary nor her father realize Hartwell hunts a blackmailer, and shouldn't waste time seeking Mary's smiles…

Miss Preston's Predicament

A Hesitant Mediums story

It was a truth universally ignored, most principally by the dowager Dame Hartwell, that ghosts and gatherings did not mix.

In this short story, the fashionable and eccentric dowager Dame Hartwell has lured the reclusive Miss Tessa Preston to attend her drawing room séance. If Dame Hartwell can't convince Miss Preston, her former protégé, to return as her medium-in-residence, she doesn't know how she will protect her son and his new fiancée from the brewing storm of malcontent spirits surrounding them.

MISS PRESTON'S PREDICAMENT is a short story between novels. It is a standalone referencing characters and events from the cozy Victorian fantasy romance, HAUNTING MISS TRENTWOOD, the first in the Hesitant Mediums series.

A Spirited Engagement
Book 2 of the Hesitant Mediums

It was a truth universally acknowledged that ghost brides are annoying romantic rivals.

Making her reluctant return to London after a ten-year absence, Tessa Preston cannot hide her dismay at her employer's friendliness with Jasper Steele, the man who chased her away. To make matters more annoying, he's haunted by a *most insistent* ghost bride.

Determined to prove her indifference to the charming Jasper, Tessa realizes the entitled ghost demanding his attention may not be all she seems. Meanwhile, unaware of Tessa's enmity, Jasper is delighted to have a second chance at her affections, and will let nothing, not even her cold stares, dampen his enthusiasm.

A SPIRITED ENGAGEMENT is a standalone romantic fantasy featuring characters from the cozy Victorian fantasy romance, HAUNTING MISS TRENTWOOD, the first in the Hesitant Mediums series.

The Last April
An Ohio Civil War Novel

Spontaneous, fifteen-year-old Gretchen vows to help heal the nation from the recently ended Civil War. On the morning of President Lincoln's death, Gretchen finds an amnesiac Confederate in her garden and believes this is her chance for civic goodwill.

But reconciliation is not as simple as Gretchen assumed. When her mother returns from the market with news that a Confederate murdered the president, Gretchen wonders if she caught the killer. Tensions between her aunt and mother rise as Gretchen nurses her Confederate prisoner, revealing secrets from their past that make Gretchen question everything she knows about loyalty, honor, and trust.

THE LAST APRIL is an entertaining, thoughtful slice-of-life novella of Ohio after the Civil War, meant to encourage teen readers to reflect on themes of fear and hope in uncertain times.

About the Author

Belinda Kroll writes sweet and cozy Victorian fantasy and fiction. Think Jane Austen-lite vocabulary meets modern sass. She is a user experience design professional, hobbyist photographer, and lindy hopper.

Kroll is obsessed with eyeglasses, Korean dramas, home renovation and cooking shows, and petting every dog that allows her to do so. She has a line of stationery for writers, readers, and creatives at Bright Bird Press. She lives with her family in Ohio.

Website https://worderella.com
Instagram https://instagram.com/worderella
Patron community https://worderella.com/community
Bright Bird Press stationery https://brightbirdpress.com